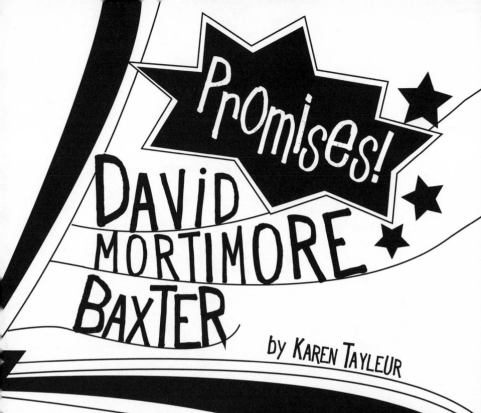

Promises!

DAVID MORTIMORE BAXTER

by KAREN TAYLEUR

illustrated by Brann Garvey

Librarian Reviewer

Kathleen Baxter

Children's Literature Consultant

formerly with Anoka County Library, MN

BA College of Saint Catherine, St. Paul, MN

MA in Library Science, University of Minnesota

Reading Consultant

Elizabeth Stedem

Educator/Consultant, Colorado Springs, CO

MA in Elementary Education, University of Denver, CO

STONE ARCH BOOKS

Minneapolis   San Diego

First published in the United States in 2007
by Stone Arch Books, A Capstone Imprint
151 Good Counsel Drive, P.O. Box 669,
Mankato, Minnesota 56002.
www.capstonepub.com

Published by arrangement with Black Dog Books.

Library of Congress Cataloging-in-Publication Data
Tayleur, Karen.
    Promises!: Vote for David Mortimore Baxter / by Karen Tayleur; illustrated
by Brann Garvey.
    p. cm. — (David Mortimore Baxter)
    Summary: To prevent the election of his old nemesis, Rose Thornton, David
Mortimore Baxter runs for class office but soon finds himself overwhelmed by campaign
promises.
    ISBN-13: 978-1-59889-076-1 (hardcover)
    ISBN-10: 1-59889-076-X (hardcover)
    ISBN-13: 978-1-59889-208-6 (paperback)
    ISBN-10: 1-59889-208-8 (paperback)
    [1. Elections—Fiction. 2. Promises—Fiction. 3. Schools—Fiction. 4. Humorous
stories.] I. Garvey, Brann, ill. II. Title. III. Title: Vote for David Mortimore Baxter. IV.
Series: Tayleur, Karen. David Mortimore Baxter.
PZ7.T21149Pr 2007
[Fic]—dc22   2006005076

Art Director: Heather Kindseth
Graphic Designer: Kay Fraser

Photo Credits
Delaney Photography, cover

Printed in the United States of America in Stevens Point, Wisconsin.
072013
007610R

Table of Contents

CHAPTER 1

THE PROMISE

So here's the thing.

Luke Firth was our class PRESIDENT. We voted for him at the beginning of the year. Everyone likes Luke. The teachers do. Even the girls. So things were going along without a problem until Luke spoiled it. That was the day he announced that he was leaving Bays Park. Which meant that **we needed a new class president**, fast. That's when things got **a little crazy**.

When Rose Thornton found out that Luke was moving, she smiled. She didn't stop smiling. I knew what she was thinking: Rose Thornton for class president. **I couldn't think of anyone worse**. I don't know if I've mentioned this before, but I really, really, really don't like Rose Thornton.

I asked **Joe Pagnopolous**, my best friend, if he'd be class president. He thought about it for two seconds.

"**No way**," he said. "You have to give speeches and stuff. You know I can't do that."

Joe is going to be an actor. But he gets sick just thinking about acting in front of other peopie. That's why he's going to be in movies. He likes to dress like **his favorite movie character**, which changes every couple of days. Today he was wearing a large pair of gray ears. Joe was also a member of a secret club called **the Secret Club** (because we hadn't thought of the perfect name yet).

BEC, my other best friend and **Secret Club member**, said she wouldn't be class president if you paid her.

"Do class presidents get paid?" I asked.

"No," she said.

I said I'd vote for Bec anyway. But Joe said that wouldn't work. "Don't you remember?" he said. "**We** nominate someone to be class president."

"Nominate?" I repeated.

"You put up your hand and say, 'I think Bec Trigg should be class president.' Then Ms. Stacey asks Bec if she wants to be class president."

"Bec would NEVER say yes," I said.

"Exactly," said Joe. "If the person says yes, Ms. Stacey puts their name on the board. There's usually a whole list of people that have been nominated. Then we have a week to decide who would be the best class president. Then we VOTE."

"The way things are going, we'll **only** have Rose Thornton to choose from," I said.

"She needs to be nominated first," said Joe.

Of course Rose would be nominated. Rose has this whole gang of girls who follow her around. One of her Giggling Girls — the **GG's** — would nominate her for sure.

"Maybe it won't be so bad having Rose as class president," said Joe.

"Maybe," I said.

Just then, Rose cruised over and slapped her hand on my desk.

"*Hey, Liar,*" she said. That's one of her special names for me. My real name is **David Mortimore Baxter**, but my friends just call me David. "When I'm class president, I'm going to make late students go straight to the hot seat."

I'm always late to class. Don't ask me why. It just happens that way. The hot seat is the seat right outside Principal Wood's office. You do 𝕹𝕺𝕿 want to be sitting there at any time.

"You can't do that," I said to Rose.

"And I'll be banning **Smashing Smorgan** pencil cases," she said, pointing to my pencil case.

"You **can't** do that," said Joe loudly, his gray ears wobbling fiercely.

"And costumes," Rose said to Joe. "Who are you today, anyway? *The Easter Bunny?*"

"She CAN'T do that, can she, David?" asked Joe, ignoring her.

I shook my head, but I wasn't sure.

Bec sneezed to let us know Ms. Stacey was coming. BEC was **famous** for her **sneezes** and **spitballs.**

"And I'll be _banning fake sneezes,_" said Rose. "Yes, things sure are going to _change_ around here." Then she walked off with a grin on her face.

"David, **you've got to run** for **class president.** There's no knowing what Rose will do if she's elected," Joe whispered.

I nodded slowly. **He was right.** We needed someone to **stand up** to Rose. It looked like no one else wanted the job.

"**I'll do it,**" I said.

"Promise?" Joe asked.

"**Promise,**" I said.

CHAPTER 2

THE NOMINATIONS

At the end of the day, Ms. Stacey asked for class president nominations.

Kaya Cheung put her hand up. "I *nominate Rose Thornton*," she said. There was applause from the GG's.

"Do you accept the nomination, Rose?" asked Ms. Stacey.

Rose Thornton stood up slowly. "*I accept the nomination*," she said, in a **loud, trembling voice**. The GG's cheered as Rose's name was written on the board.

"Are there any **further** nominations?" asked Ms. Stacey. She looked around the room.

"*No one else?*" she said, looking disappointed.

It was quiet. I could hear our science project growing at the back of the room.

"If there's no one else," Ms. Stacey finally said, "then we're all set."

"I nominate David Baxter," said Bec loudly. She looked over at me. I nodded at her.

Ms. Stacey looked like she was about to 𝔽𝔸𝕀ℕ𝕋. "Do you accept the nomination, David?" she whispered weakly.

I stood up. "**I do,**" I said loudly.

There were **cheers** from the back of the room. I waved to my fans and sat down. It was **pretty cool**.

Ms. Stacey added my name to the board. "Any more nominations?" asked Ms. Stacey. She seemed to really want another name. But no one else raised their hand. "Okay," she said, "**ten days** from **today** we'll have our **class president election**. I don't want Luke to leave his job before he has to."

Then the bell rang. Some people came over and slapped me on the back.

"Good one, David."

"Awesome!"

"**Nice one.**"

I felt Rose Thornton's **stare burning my skin.**

I felt like an ant under a magnifying glass. I smiled wider.

The next day in class, Ms. Stacey was her old self again.

"I thought we'd have a little fun with our election process," she said.

We all GROANED. By "fun," Ms. Stacey usually meant "WORK."

Ms. Stacey wrote the word "election" on the board. Then she asked what it meant.

Jake Davern was throwing his arm around in the air. Finally Ms. Stacey chose him. "It's when you really like something, like monkeys," he said.

Everyone laughed.

Ms. Stacey wrote "ELECTION" bigger on the board, then underlined it.

"Election, Jake. Not affection," she said.

Joe was doing **a snorty** little laugh that I'd never heard before. He was still wearing his grey ears.

Maybe it was part of his character. I PUNCHED him to be quiet.

Ms. Stacey wrote the word "democracy" on the board. Then she explained that we have elections in our country, because it is a *democratic society*. Which means that everyone gets one vote to choose who is going to be the leader.

Joe put up his hand.

"Yes, Joe?" asked Ms. Stacey.

"So, once I VOTE for David, he wins," said Joe.

"Everyone gets a vote, Joe," explained Ms. Stacey. "Then the votes are *counted*. The person with the most votes wins."

"So, if Rose gets MORE votes than David, David loses?" asked Joe.

"*Exactly*," said Ms. Stacey.

"Then I **wasted** my vote," complained Joe.

"So just vote for Rose," someone called out. Everyone laughed.

"Let's talk about election campaigns," said Ms. Stacey. She talked about how politicians go around and talk to the voters. And *how they make speeches and kiss babies and make promises.*

"I don't have to **kiss any babies**, do I?" I asked Joe.

Joe shook his long gray ears.

I had to ask. "**What's with the ears**, Joe?"

"I just saw a movie about an **ogre**. It was **great**," said Joe.

"But ogres don't have long gray ears," I said.

"I know," he said. "**I'm the wise donkey.**"

Ms. Stacey assigned us a project to do on elections and voting. She gave us five minutes to choose a group. Bec came over and joined Joe and me.

"This is good," said Joe. "**Let's run a campaign** to get David elected as class president. We can do it in class."

I looked at Luke Firth. He seemed a little sad. His class president badge was **gold** and **shiny** on his chest.

"I want to do the posters," said Bec. "And some 'Vote for David' stickers." Bec was really good at anything to do with art.

"Well, I'm going to be the **campaign manager**," said Joe.

"What does a campaign manager do?" I asked.

"I'm not sure," said Joe. "But I've always wanted to be a manager. **I want people to start taking me seriously.**"

"Can I make a suggestion?" asked Bec.

"Sure," said Joe.

"You want people to take you **seriously**? I'd **lose those long ears** if I were you."

CHAPTER 3

THE PLAN

That night, Joe called me **six times** to talk about the election.

"Tell Joe you're eating dinner," said Mom as I answered the sixth call.

When I got back to the dinner table, Mom wanted to know what Joe's problem was. I explained about the election.

"**You**? Class president?" said my little brother, Harry. "**Are you crazy?**"

Once I would have agreed with him. I liked just sitting in class with Joe. No need to worry about making speeches. Or setting an example. But maybe it was time for a change.

"I think it **builds character**," said Dad. "**Good job**, David."

My sister, Zoe, GRUNTED.

The next morning there were Rose Thornton posters all over the walls in our classroom. There were even some in the cafeteria and the bathrooms — girls' and boys'.

"It's just WRONG," said Joe. "I can't do anything in the bathroom with Rose Thornton's face in there. It's like she's watching me."

"I wouldn't be surprised if cafeteria sales dropped," added Bec.

I held up a sticker that read, "Vote For Rose Thornton for Class President"

"She sure has been BUSY," I said.

Then James Goh tapped me on the shoulder. "Rose Thornton promised me a Meal Deal from Chunky Chicken if I vote for her and she wins," he said.

"I don't believe it!" said Bec.

"So, I'm wondering what you're going to promise," James said.

I looked at Joe, who stepped forward. "As David's campaign manager," he said, "I'm here to tell you that **we'll match any promise** that Rose Thornton makes — **plus more.**"

"**What!**" I yelled.

"**Cool**," said James. "I don't want to vote for Rose, but, well, you know." Then he ran away.

"Joe, **I can't afford to do that**," I began.

That's when Joe opened the notebook he was holding. **He must have spent all night working on it.** In the middle of the page was a huge circle. Inside the circle were the words "**Core Promises**." Outside the circle were smaller circles labeled "**Promises**." There were other labels like "**Might Keep**," and "**Should Keep**."

Joe pointed to one of the smaller circles. "We just made James a promise," he explained. Then he pointed to the larger circle. "But it wasn't a **Core Promise**."

"**But a promise is a promise**," I said.

Joe shook his head. "**NOT** in elections," he said. "I watched a movie about it last night. Let me explain. Say you promise to do something. Then, if you get elected, you don't do it. Well, that's okay. That happens all the time. Voters understand that. But if you make a **core promise**, voters expect you to keep that. Unless something comes up that means you really can't keep it."

"So a promise isn't really a promise at all?" asked Bec.

"**NOT** in elections," said Joe.

"But isn't that **wrong**?" I asked.

Joe explained. He'd had a really long talk with his dad the night before. Mr. P. explained the way elections worked. Promises and core promises. You do anything it takes to win.

I was still trying to work it all out when Jake Davern came up. Rose had talked to him about a Meal Deal offer, too.

Rose was walking around the school like she'd already won the election. Joe and I were talking about the latest match on **World Wrestling Mania** when Kaya Cheung came over and sat next to me. She gave Joe a little wave. **I watched his ears turn red.**

"Do you have a campaign manager, David?" asked Kaya.

"**Yeah, me**," said Joe.

"I have something for you," she said, handing an envelope to Joe. Then she ran off GIGGLING.

Joe **opened it carefully**, like the envelope **might explode at any moment**. Inside was a note that looked official.

"What does it say?" I demanded.

"Rose Thornton wants to **have a debate** before the election."

"**No way**," I said.

"You **have to**," explained Joe. "If you don't, people will think you have **something to hide**."

"But Rose uses **big words**," I said. "She'll try and trick me. She'll probably get her MOTHER to **write her speech**."

"Don't worry," said Joe. "We just need to figure out Rose's **main points** and have some answers ready. It'll be easy."

This from a kid who throws up before he goes onstage.

A **debate** with Rose Thornton. Could I possibly imagine **anything worse**?

NO.

CHAPTER 4

FRAMED

That night I couldn't sleep. The more I thought about it, the more I wasn't sure I wanted to be class president. I didn't even know how I got into that mess. I felt pretty bad for Joe and Bec. They'd worked hard on my campaign. But once I decided to let Rose Thornton be class president, I felt better. That's how I knew it was the right thing to do.

The next morning I got to school early. I wanted to find Rose Thornton and tell her before Joe and Bec could change my mind. The first person I saw was Jake Davern.

"Hey, Jake," I called out.

Jake stood still and looked at me. Finally he turned and walked away. He didn't even wave. I shrugged. Jake was a nutcase. Who knew what went on in his head?

The next person I saw was the crossing lady.

Usually she's got A LOT to say. Telling me to keep my toes off the road until she blows the whistle. Commanding me to have a good day. Like I have control over that. Today she just frowned and blew her whistle sharply in my ear.

"Have a good day," I said.

"Keep walking," she barked.

I saw Sam Beavis next. He was reading something on the noticeboard.

"Morning, Sam," I yelled.

Sam looked at me, then shook his head. "Loser," he said.

"What?" I yelled as he walked away.

I looked at the noticeboard. Stuck in the middle was a huge poster. A large black heading read, "Is this your next class president?" There was a CREEPY photo of me. I'd done my usual squinty photo smile, which makes me look like I have something to hide. Someone had added two devil horns to the top of my head in pen.

Class Clown/Liar — David Mortimore Baxter — was the last person seen playing with Banjo, our beloved school cat. Since Friday, no one has seen Banjo. His food lies untouched. His litter remains clear. Who knows what terrible thing has happened to our innocent kitten? Rose Thornton, candidate for the upcoming class president election for Ms. Stacey's class, had this to say: "If I am elected class president, I will stamp out animal cruelty. People shouldn't be able to get away with things like this." There has been no comment from David Mortimore Baxter or his campaign manager, Joe Pagnopoolous.

I read the poster TWICE before I understood what it meant. Rose was saying, without saying it, that I'd done something mean to Banjo. No wonder no one wanted to talk me. **They thought I was hurting the cat.** I was reading the poster a third time when Joe arrived. He held a copy of the poster.

"**Now I'm mad,**" he said.

"**They can't write those things about me. Can they, Joe?**" I asked.

"**Pagnopoolous**? Poo? They have gone too far," he said, **shaking his fist**. He grabbed the poster from the noticeboard. "Let's just see what Ms. Stacey has to say about this."

If I thought Joe was mad, Ms. Stacey was even MADDER. "Okay," was all she said. Then she shooed us out of the classroom.

By the time school started, people were staying away from me, like they might catch something. Joe and Bec were the only ones to walk into class with me. I noticed Rose Thornton talking to Ms. Stacey. Rose was looking very serious. **Boy, was she in trouble.**

Ms. Stacey clapped her hands to get everyone's attention. "Okay, everyone," she said. "Rose would like to say a few words."

Rose held the cat poster up for everyone to see. "I don't know if everyone has seen this poster," she began.

There was an **angry murmur** through the class. Someone actually hissed.

"I would just like to say — for the record — that I *had nothing to do with this poster*. I checked with Mr. Edwards, the school cleaner. He told me that **Banjo** is **well** and **safe**. I am appalled that someone would try to hurt my opponent's chances of winning. I am here for a *fair fight* and I hope you don't hold this against David."

The class started clapping, then went WILD when Rose came over and shook my hand.

"*Good luck, David*," she said **loudly**. Then, in a whisper, she added, "You too, *Poo*."

I knew it! Rose Thornton had set me up. And she'd ended up looking like a hero.

I smiled — a huge, fake smile. "You are going down, Rose Thornton," I said quietly.

And suddenly *I was back in the race.*

CHAPTER 5

THE LIST

After school we had a **Secret Club** meeting. Bec brought her pet rat, **Ralph**, who was also a club member, and The **Secret Club Book** to take notes. We had the meeting in the study and Boris pushed his way in before we could shut the door. We told Mom that we were doing homework and to keep Harry out. Harry was always trying to do whatever I was doing. Having a little brother can be really annoying.

Mom had made us some after-school munchies. There were **weird things** with **blueberries** (Bec thought they might be muffins) and **milkshakes**. We fed a weird thing to Boris, who ate it **in one gulp**. Ralph picked at the crumbs. We waited five minutes. **When neither pet died, we started eating.**

"I think we should start," Joe said. "I call this meeting to order."

Ever since the election was announced, Joe was different. He used to be GOOFY and kind of weird. Joe was always pretending to be someone, or something, that he wasn't. I wondered what movie he'd watched. He'd changed from likeable, nutty Joe to smart, hardcore Joe.

"I've got a **few ideas**," he said.

Joe wanted me to talk to every person in our class, including the **GG's**. That is what **politicians** did.

"The **GG's** are never going to vote for me," I said.

But Joe said you could NEVER be sure.

"What do I talk about?" I asked.

"All you need to do is figure out what people are interested in and talk about that," said Joe. "Here. I made a **list of suggestions**."

<u>Class List</u>

Beavis, Sam..........football

Chatfield, William.......cars

Cheung, Kaya.......girl things?

Chui, Tom.......trading cards

Davern, Jake.......monkeys

D'Amelio, Alexander.......baseball

Debono, Louis.......art

Devine, Alysha.......girl things

Ellis, Stephanie.......reading

Ellul, Katerina.......music

Farmer, Jordan.......wrestling

Firth, Luke.......don't worry about (leaving)

Garcia, Stefan.......wrestling

Goh, James.......wrestling (don't worry, promised Chunky Chicken)

Hall, Lee.......scary movies

Irvine, Bonnie.......girl things

Johnson, Carly.......makeup

Jurkovic, Paul.......surfing

Lang, Chris.......basketball

Lee, Lily.......*designer clothes*

McKenzie, Brianna.......*music*

Nagy, Kelli.......*girl things*

Osborne, Gemma.......*sports*

Pagnopolous, Joe.......*don't worry about* (*manager*)

Phung, Mitch.......*cars*

Reynolds, Joshua.......*scary things*

Savoia, Rudy.......*magic tricks*

Thompson, Chase.......*collecting bottle tops*

Thornton, Rose.......*ignore*

Trigg, Rebecca.......*art* (*don't worry about*)

Van Veen, Elly.......*reading*

Webb, Blake.......*sports*

"That's great, Joe," I said.

Bec scribbled in the Club Book, "Class list suggestion from Joe accepted."

Ralph scrambled up my arm and sat on my shoulder. I offered him a **crumb**.

Bec pulled a camera out of her backpack. "Smile!" she said. "That'll make a great publicity shot for the school newsletter. For when David wins," she explained.

Joe nodded. "Good idea."

"What am I going to talk about in the debate?" I asked. I was feeling LOST.

"The usual stuff," said Joe. "How you're the man for the job. How you will be dedicated. How you have great ideas and plans for the future."

Then Boris got up and stretched himself.

"What is that smell?" moaned Bec.

Boris looked GUILTY.

"Meeting over," said Joe. We all ran for the door.

As we left, Boris gobbled down **another muffin.**

* * *

The next day at school, I studied the list. It was way too long. And how could I talk about girl things?

Maybe I should ask Bec. Suddenly a football stamped with the words "**Bays Park**" landed right in the middle of the list. The ball's stitching was unraveling. It looked like it might have been the first football ever made.

Sam Beavis came over and grabbed the ball.

"Sorry," he said.

At least he was talking to me again. I checked my list. Sam Beavis — football.

"So you really like football?" I asked.

Sam tossed the ball in the air. "Sure," he said.

"What if I promised to stock the sports locker with twenty new footballs if I'm elected class president?" I asked.

"Wow! That'd be cool," said Sam. "You've got my vote."

Then he ran off, holding the ball under his arm.

I placed a check next to Sam's name. One down, 26 to go.

That day I talked to five more people. I used the football promise on Alexander and Stefan. I promised Jake Davern that our class would **sponsor a monkey** at the zoo. And I promised Jordan Farmer that I'd get him some FREE tickets to a taping of **World Wrestling Mania**. Six kids down, 21 to go.

At the end of the day, **Victor Sneddon** was waiting at the front door of the school.

"**Hey you**," he said, pointing a finger the size of a large salami at me.

I looked around, but everyone seemed to have scattered. Did I mention that Victor is Rose Thornton's cousin and the official school bully?

I pointed a finger to my chest and he nodded. Victor and I go way back. I moved a little closer to him and he scowled.

"**Come here**," he said.

I moved closer.

"You're running for class president in Ms. Stacey's class?" he asked.

I nodded.

"So's Rose," he said.

I nodded again.

"Rose **really wants to be class president**," he grumbled. "So you better make sure that happens. **Understand?**"

I nodded once more.

"I can't hear you," he said, smiling wickedly.

"**Yes**," I SQUEAKED.

"Good," said Victor. "I'm glad we understand each other."

I looked up and saw Ms. Stacey watching us. Victor must have seen her too because **he punched my arm in a playful way.**

"Now **get outta here**," he said.

CHAPTER 6

THE DEAL

At dinner, Mom mentioned that she'd talked to Rose Thornton's mother on the phone.

"I didn't realize you were running for **class president**, Davey," said Mom.

She said that Mrs. Thornton said that it would be good for Rose to be class president. Mrs. Thornton said that it would BOOST Rose's self-confidence. Dad said he didn't think Rose Thornton had a problem with that. Personally, I thought Rose Thornton had a problem with self-confidence. She had too much!

"Davey, why did you decide to run for **class president?**" asked Mom.

Because Rose Thornton would make a DUMB class president? Because I didn't want to spend every day on the hot seat? Because I liked my Smashing Smorgan pencil case and wanted to use it at school?

These were all true, but I wasn't sure how these reasons would go down with Mom. I tried to think of some other ideas.

"I think it would be good for my **self-confidence**," I said, copying Mrs. Thornton. "I think I'm the 𝕄𝔸ℕ for the job," I said. "I will be a dedicated class president. I've got some great ideas and plans for the future."

Zoe raised her eyebrows and Harry **blew bubbles** in his drink. But Mom and Dad looked impressed.

"That's very commendable, David. I see you've really thought about this," said Dad.

"Yeah," I said, warming to the idea. "And I think kids like me. In fact, they pretty much **begged me** to be **class president**. And I'm pretty good at keeping secrets, sometimes. I want to make sure we have the best class in the school." I stood up. "And I want to 𝕎𝕆ℝ𝕂 with Ms. Stacey to help make that happen."

"That's not going to happen," whined Harry. "My class is the best class in the school."

But no one listened.

Mom and Dad CLAPPED and Boris BARKED from under the table. Zoe thumped the table. I did a little bow and sat down in my seat.

And tried not to think about **Victor Sneddon.**

* * *

After I helped Zoe with the dishes, I visited Harry's bedroom. This is not a place you want to hang out. It smells horrible, like Harry. A **combination of moldy fruit and Boris's fur.**

Harry was lying on his bed and looking at his trading cards.

"I want to make a deal with you," I said.

"What?" said Harry, not looking up.

"I'm pretty busy running for class president and everything," I said.

"So?" said Harry.

"So I was wondering if you'd **do my chores** until this is all over."

"Sure," said Harry.

"Really?" I asked.

"**Nope**," said Harry.

"Come on, Harry," I said.

"Why would I want to do **your chores** and mine?" asked Harry.

"Because when I'm class president, **I'll do all your chores for four days**."

"A week," said Harry.

"Five days," I said.

"Six," said Harry.

"**Promise?**" I asked.

"**Promise**," said Harry.

We sealed the deal with a **spit high-five**.

"The chores list is on the inside of the pantry door," I said as I left.

"**Nice doing business with you**," said Harry.

The next day was SATURDAY — the best day of the week. I decided to ask Zoe to coach me for my debate with Rose. Zoe had been on the school debate team. Also, she was pretty good at putting people in their place. I had to wait until she got out of bed before I could ask her. By 11 a.m. I was bored with waiting. I made a lot of noise in the kitchen. Zoe finally appeared.

"Good morning," I said. I poured her a juice and she grunted a thanks. I followed her into the living room. I watched her sip her juice and flip the channels on the TV.

I was trying to figure out the best time to ask, when she finally said, "What?"

"I need help debating Rose," I said.

She flipped through some more channels.

"Why do you want to be class president?" she finally demanded.

"Because the only other CHOICE was Rose Thornton and I didn't want it to be her," I said.

Zoe nodded. "What do I get out of it?" she asked.

"Maybe I could help you with your homework? Or something," I said.

A little smile crept onto her face. "Do you promise?" she asked.

"Sure," I said.

We SPIT into our hands and slapped a high-five.

"Deal," we said.

Zoe spent the next hour giving me TIPS about **debating**. She showed me how to write up **little cards** of information to help keep the ideas in my head. She showed me how to grip onto something steady with both hands. That way, no one could see my hands shake if I was nervous. She taught me to pick out something on the wall at the back of the room and look at that while I was speaking. She also said, if I was really nervous, I could IMAGINE that everyone in the room was just **wearing their underwear.**

I shook my head. "That is just too disgusting," I said.

"You're right," she said. "Well, I think you're just about ready."

"Thanks, Zoe. You're the best."

"I know," she said. "Now you can help me with my homework."

"Can I just get something to eat first?" I asked.

"Sure. I'll just get everything ready," she said.

I got some cookies and grabbed a **glass of milk** from the fridge. When I walked back into the living room, Zoe was messing around with some **black material**.

She held up a half-finished **dress**. "Put it on."

CHAPTER 7

I AM DEAD

I laughed and dunked a **cookie into my milk.**

"Yeah, right."

"David. *I'm serious.* Put the dress on. I need to pin up the hem and take in a few tucks."

I shook my head. "No way. **That's a dress,**" I said.

"I know what it is," she said firmly.

"**I'm a boy,**" I said, like maybe she'd forgotten.

"Put the dress on, David," she said.

"No!"

"You *made a promise.* Now put it on."

"**No way!**" I said. I MEANT it.

"If you don't, I'm telling Mom that it was Boris who destroyed her herb garden last weekend. And not a **wild coyote with large fangs** like you said," said Zoe.

Mom was still angry about losing her herbs. I wasn't so sure she'd believed the coyote story anyway. Actually, Boris can look like a wild coyote sometimes. Well, only if you SQUINT your eyes really hard. In the dark.

"It'll only take five minutes," Zoe said. "You can use my cell phone for a day," she added.

Ten minutes later I was standing on the coffee table in the living room, watching Double Trouble, and wearing a DRESS. I was pretty safe. Harry was at football with Mom and Dad, and Zoe had closed the curtains.

I'd pretty much forgotten I was wearing a dress when the doorbell rang. I didn't even notice when Zoe left to answer the door. The next thing I knew, there was a murmur of voices and the living room door swung open.

"Who is it?" I whispered.

Zoe dug around in a drawer. "Just some kids fund raising for something. I'm sure I saw some money in here the other day."

"Shut the door," I hissed.

"It's okay," said Zoe. "*They can't see you.*" She pulled out a gold coin. "Coming," she yelled out.

There was the sound of footsteps in the hallway and suddenly three faces appeared at the door. Three familiar faces. Three girls from Ms. Stacey's class. I turned around quickly and faced the TV, hoping they hadn't seen me.

"I said I was coming," said Zoe.

The girls just GIGGLED.

"Sorry," said one. It sounded like Bonnie Irvine. "I thought you said, 'come in.' Is that you, David?"

I thought I might pretend to be someone else, but Zoe said, "David's just helping me with a *school project*. For sewing."

"AWW," said the girl who sounded like Bonnie. "That's sweet. Isn't that SWeet?"

The other girls agreed. They came over for a closer look at Zoe's black dress and my RED face.

Sure enough, it was Bonnie Irvine with Carly Johnson and Kaya Cheung — three of Rose's GG's.

"This is a cool dress, Zoe. Do you have a pattern?"

Zoe babbled about how she didn't have a pattern and how she was going to be a designer. How she loved working with the **color black**. How it was going to be **her signature color** (whatever that meant). I wanted to escape but there were fifty million pins sticking into the dress. I couldn't make a move without becoming a VOODOO DOLL. Finally the girls left and Zoe kept pinning the dress like nothing had happened.

"Thanks a lot!" I yelled.

"What?" asked Zoe.

"Those girls SAW me in this dress!"

I was so angry I could hardly speak.

"They seemed *perfectly nice*," said Zoe. "Anyway, it's not my fault they saw you. It's not like I asked them in."

"I will NEVER live this down. Forget about me being class president. Or getting any older. Once everyone knows, I'm dead meat."

"Dribbles, you're SO dramatic sometimes," said Zoe. "Now stay still."

"I am dead. I am dead. I am dead," I chanted, until Zoe stuck me with a pin and I stopped. "This is the worst thing that has ever happened to me — that will ever happen to me – in my entire life," I grumbled.

As usual, **I was wrong**.

CHAPTER 8

On Sunday, Joe and Bec came around and we hung out in the park for a while. The day was nice enough. The sun was shining and we did some **major spying** on Mr. McCafferty, my neighbor. Mr. M. was digging in his front garden.

"What do you think he's doing?" Bec asked.

"Probably **burying a body,**" I said. I had this theory about Mr. McCafferty. Mr. McCafferty and his house filled with newspaper piles. Mr. McCafferty and his obsession with watching **medical shows**. But that's another story.

"I thought you were supposed to be **watering his plants,**" said Joe.

I nodded. "He's leaving today for his vacation. He offered to pay me, but Mom said it was the least we could do. I was with her at the time. She nudged me, so **I promised** a day wouldn't go by without the plants being watered."

"I was thinking I might get a chance to take a look around without him being there. Anyway, now it's **Harry's problem**." I explained about Harry taking over my chores.

"What did you do yesterday?" asked Bec.

Somehow I couldn't tell Bec and Joe about the dress thing. It was just **too embarrassing**. Also, Joe was in a good mood about the election and I didn't want to spoil his fun.

"Nothing much. I think it might be lunchtime," I said, changing the subject.

Sunday is the day Gran comes to lunch. My gran is deaf when she wants to be. She has three whiskers on her chin. And she drives a sports car — really slowly. Sunday lunch is always a big deal at our house.

We left the park and found Dad extending the dining table at home. More people were coming.

"Are Joe and Bec staying for lunch?" asked Dad.

"Uh-huh. When's lunch? **I'm starving,**" I said.

"As soon as the guests arrive!"

"Who else is coming?" I asked.

"**The Thornton family**," said Dad cheerfully.

How to RUIN a Sunday in one easy step. Invite Rose Thornton over for Sunday lunch. Dad and Mr. Thornton were good friends. Dad was always finding ways for the Thorntons and the Baxters to get together.

"Suddenly I'm not so hungry," I mumbled as the doorbell rang.

"Please answer the door, David," said Dad as **loud banging** began on the door.

Bec and Joe followed me. I opened the door. I got a whack on my shin from Gran's walking stick. She'd been using it to bang the door.

"I've been out here for at least twenty minutes," she complained. "Does that doorbell work?" She peered at Joe and Bec like they were some interesting bugs. "Don't you two have a home?" she asked.

Joe laughed a nervous LAUGH and Bec sneezed. Joe and Bec were used to Gran's weird ways.

Then Gran BARGED in and shoved a large, brown paper bag at me, saying, "Take this. Your mother tells me you're in an election. We'll talk later." Then she sailed into the kitchen. Her stick didn't even touch the ground.

I looked inside the bag. It was just some **old blue coat** with lines on it. I left it on the floor.

"Let's go to your place," I whispered to Joe, but it was too late.

The Thorntons had pulled up in their SHINY new car. Mrs. Thornton waved at us.

"Hello there," she called out **cheerfully**. Mrs. Thornton has this way of talking to me **like I'm three years old**.

I waved back.

Things were going pretty **smoothly**. Mom had made a roast, which is one thing she can cook. Rose Thornton sat between her mother and Zoe. Joe, Bec, and I sat at the other end of the table. Rose had spent most of the time before lunch texting friends on her cellphone. The only person she talked to was Zoe.

"Zoe, Rose tells me you design your own clothes," said Mrs. Thornton.

I felt my insides freeze. Rose probably knew about the dress. But Rose just kept eating and didn't look up. I prayed Zoe wouldn't say anything stupid. She didn't. She just talked about her sewing class.

"Well, I think that's wonderful," said Mrs. Thornton. "It's a pity you don't have time to design a victory dress for Rose."

"A what?" said Zoe.

"A victory dress. For when Rose becomes president." Suddenly, Mrs. Thornton looked embarrassed. She shoveled some food into her mouth. "Delicious, Cordelia, just delicious," she said.

I looked over at Mom, who had stopped eating. Dad chimed in. "That's right. Rose and David are both running for class president," he said. "Well, may the best man win."

"Or woman," said Mrs. Thornton with a sniff.

"Or woman," agreed Dad, CHUCKLING.

"Where's that bag?" interrupted Gran. "Where is it, David?"

She meant the paper bag. I left the dining table and grabbed it from the hallway.

"*Bring it here*," commanded Gran. She pulled a suit jacket out of the bag. It had a **funny smell**, like she'd **found it in a museum**. She pushed it at me. "Try it on," she said.

I put the jacket on. The sleeves hung down and completely hid my hands. The jacket came down to **my knees**.

Gran nodded her approval. "*Perfect*," she said, tapping me on the chest. "David Mortimore Baxter, *your grandfather* wore this when he became President of the Finefellows Historical Society on September 19, 1957. This is what *you will be wearing when you become* **class president** *on Wednesday*," she announced.

Mr. Thornton gave a **nervous cough**. Mrs. Thornton looked annoyed and spoke loudly to Gran because sometimes Gran's **a little deaf**.

She said maybe it was time for a female class president. That really, no offense to David or his family, Rose was probably the better choice. Rose was mature and had a pleasant manner.

Rose was nodding like she agreed with every word.

"Please!" said Gran. "The job should go to the best person available. And that person is my grandson!"

"Mother!" said Dad.

"Anyone for more dessert?" asked Mom brightly.

"Well, we all know that David is unstable," said Mrs. Thornton.

"Now, wait a minute!" said Mom.

"But Cordelia, it's true! All that lying and sneaking around."

Rose looked uncomfortable. She wasn't above a little lying and sneaking around of her own.

"Davey doesn't lie," said Mom. "He just bends the truth sometimes."

Joe KICKED me under the table. I looked over at Rose and pointed to the door.

Joe, Bec, Rose, and I left without anyone noticing. There was way too much **noise between the adults** arguing and Boris barking.

"I wish they wouldn't fight," said Rose. "It's **NONE** *of their business*, really."

For once I agreed with her.

CHAPTER 9

MAKING PROMISES

Ms. Stacey decided that our debate would be held in the **school hall**. This way we could use the stage and the **lectern**. I wasn't sure what a lectern was. It turned out to be **the wooden thing** that Principal Woods stood behind and rested his notes on when he was making a speech. Ms. Stacey said we would each use the lectern to make opening remarks. Then we would sit on chairs next to each other for the debate.

She also said that there would be a **little surprise** at the **end of the debate**. Jake Davern wanted to know what it was, but Ms. Stacey wouldn't tell. Finally, she said that she hoped the candidates had done their homework, because the class would be allowed to ask questions.

Luckily I'd been working on some answers to questions people might ask me. I got the **answer cards** out of my pencil case and showed them to Joe.

He shook his head. "**Forget those**," he said. "I've already written the **answers** for you."

I noticed a black briefcase at his feet. Joe was starting to look like a manager. He opened it up and handed me some cards.

"Gee, Joe, thanks," I said, looking at the cards.

"No need to thank me, David. That's what I'm here for."

I didn't know what to say, so I PUNCHED him on the arm.

"How about a game of four square at lunchtime?" I asked.

"I'd really like that," said Joe. "But the **debate's tomorrow** and the election is the next day. Have you talked to all the voters yet?"

I shook my head.

"Well, then. I don't think we really have time for four square. **Do you**?"

That's when I wished Joe was wearing his **stupid gray ears**.

"**We have got to win this**!" said Joe.

He was starting to **creep ME out**. I thought I was the one running for class president.

* * *

When the lunch bell rang, Ms. Stacey called me to her desk.

"Are you having *trouble with Victor Sneddon*?" she asked.

I shook my head. "**No, Ms. Stacey**," I said.

"I saw you two talking the other day," she said. "You didn't *look too happy*."

Well, **GEE**, I wanted to say. Maybe I wasn't happy because Victor Sneddon wanted me to make sure that Rose Thornton became **class president**. Meanwhile, my friends **were doing everything** to make sure I became class president.

"**Everything's okay**," I said. Then I went outside.

Joe sat me down under the oak tree. Then he **DELIVERED** a new kid from our class every couple of minutes.

I promised Tom Chui I'd give him some **trading cards** for his collection. "Just remember, you don't want Rose Thornton for class president," Joe told Tom. "She's going to make it a rule that everyone wears PINK."

I promised Lee Hall and Joshua Reynolds some **horror movies** from the Pagnopolous's video store. "I heard Rose Thornton is going to **get scary stories** BANNED from the library," I said.

Before the next voter arrived, **a shadow** fell over the list of promises. I looked up to see Victor Sneddon.

"I hear you're making **election promises**," said Victor.

I nodded.

"So what are you going to **promise me**?" said Victor.

"Uh," I said. "I thought you wanted Rose to be class president."

"Sure I do. Rose is my cousin," said Victor. "Also, she promised me two tickets to the football finals. So I was wondering, if you could promise me something better."

"Teacher's coming," sneezed Bec.

I looked behind Victor's shoulder. There was no one there. But Bec had given me an idea.

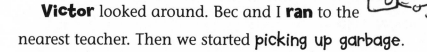

"Hello, Ms. Stacey," I yelled.

Victor looked around. Bec and I ran to the nearest teacher. Then we started picking up garbage.

"Thank you, Rebecca," said Mrs. George, our art teacher. "Goodness. Don't tell me you've turned over a new leaf, David."

Victor caught up to us. He gave me a look that said I'll get you later, then strolled off.

* * *

That night, VICTOR called.

"We didn't get to finish our conversation today," he said.

"Conversation?" I repeated. I felt a little sick. I must have been looking sick too. Zoe stopped what she was doing and asked if I was all right. I nodded.

"You know what I'm talking about," said Victor. "What you would do for me if I let you run for class president."

"Oh. That," I said, waving Zoe away.

Zoe shrugged and disappeared into her room. An awful idea came to me. The ONLY idea that made sense.

"I guess I could get you a date with my sister," I said. "You know, Zoe."

Victor Sneddon sure knew my sister. He'd had a crush on her for a year.

"Oh. Zoe. Yeah, I remember her. Wears a lot of black," said Victor.

"That's the one," I said.

"You promise?" asked Victor.

"Uh—huh," I said. I hoped Victor understood about elections and promises.

"Okay. You're ON, class president," he said. He chuckled. Then he hung up.

Zoe **poked her head out** of her bedroom door.

"Who was that?" she demanded.

"Victor Sneddon," I said.

"*Oh, him,*" said Zoe with a **snort**. "*He's a weirdo.*" Then she slammed her door again.

"**I hope you like dating weirdos,**" I whispered.

CHAPTER 10

THE DEBATE

The next day, before the debate, Mr. Woods called Rose and Ms. Stacey and me into his office. Luke Firth was already there. He waved hello as I walked in.

"We have a **small problem**," began Mr. Woods.

Luke Firth wasn't moving anymore. His mother's new job had fallen through.

"*Hey, that's great!*" I said.

Everyone else stayed quiet. There was a strange noise coming from Rose's mouth. *I think she was grinding her teeth.*

"Yes, well, I think you can see our problem," said Mr. Woods. "Technically, Luke is still class president."

"However, I think we've gone too far not to have an election," said Ms. Stacey. "We have a **debate** scheduled for this afternoon. *My students have been using this as a project. I can't just abandon the* election now."

Mr. Woods nodded. **"Yes,"** he said. 'Well, I think the debate should continue as planned. However, I will be looking into this matter further."

Ms. Stacey asked us to leave, so she could talk to Mr. Woods in private. We walked out and Rose stormed off.

"Wow," said Luke.

"She really wants to be class president," I said.

Luke nodded. He was still wearing his **class president badge.**

"What's **so good** about being class president?" I asked.

"I dunno," said Luke, touching his badge. "I guess I like **helping people.** I like **organizing things.** This is the first thing that I've ever been good at. I'm the youngest at home." He shrugged. **"No one else at home has been class president."**

I nodded.

"Why do you want to be class president?" he asked.

I didn't have an answer.

* * *

As I walked into the assembly hall that afternoon, people **laughed** and **pointed at me** as I walked to the stage. I sucked at my teeth. No leftover lunch. I **wiped my nose on my sleeve.** I checked to see if my zipper was up. Everything okay there.

I saw the poster on the wall as I reached the stage. It was the picture that Bec **had taken,** the one of me feeding her pet rat, Ralph. The printed heading read, "**David Baxter for Class President.**" But someone had written on the poster, so that it read, "**David Baxter for Class President? I smell a rat!**"

"**I'm sorry, David,**" whispered Bec from the front row. "Rose's gang must have done it."

Rose was sitting onstage with her feet together and **a smirk on her face.** Rose and I sat next to each other as we waited for everyone to arrive. Apparently Ms. Stacey had said that anyone could come to the debate. Some other classes were already filing into the hall.

There were adults too. I saw Mrs. George and Ms. Lutsky, the office lady. Then Mom arrived, alone. Thankfully there wasn't going to be a whole Baxter family show. Just as I relaxed a little, the double doors to the hall swung open and **Gran barged in.** She charged up the aisle, clearing a path with her walking stick. Ms. Stacey stepped forward, but Gran pushed her out of the way. Gran was **on a mission.**

"David," she boomed. "David Mortimore Baxter."

Gran always likes to use my whole name. I'm not sure whether it's because it was her husband's name, or if she just likes to embarrass me.

I wondered if I could ignore her. Rose leaned forward and tapped me on the knee. I could tell she was enjoying the show.

"Isn't that **your grandmother?**" she asked.

"Daaaaavvvvidddd," Gran called out.

I gave her a little wave. "Hi, Gran," I said weakly.

Gran **pushed a large paper bag** onto the stage. "*Put it on*," she commanded. I figured I'd better put it on before she came up on stage and dressed me herself.

I put on the coat. Someone had hemmed the sleeves. At least I could see my hands. I slipped my opening remarks into one pocket and Joe's notes into the other. All of a sudden **I felt different. Taller. Older.** It felt like I'd slipped on a costume and **was going to play a character.**

Gran gave an approving nod and went to find a seat.

Ms. Stacey walked onstage and went to the lectern. She tapped the microphone. "One, two," she said. "One, two . . ."

"Three, four," said someone from the audience.

LAUGHTER ran through the crowd. There were at least a hundred people seated. There were also other **people standing at the back of the hall.**

"I think we should *start*," said Ms. Stacey.

She introduced Rose Thornton as the first candidate. There was applause as Rose walked to the lectern.

I watched Rose speak, but I wasn't listening. I looked out into the crowd and saw Mrs. Thornton.

Every time the crowd APPLAUDED, she would **clap loudly**. Her lips moved as Rose spoke. She seemed to be echoing Rose's speech word for word. It seemed very important to her, not just the debate, but the whole class president thing. Suddenly, Rose picked up her papers and returned to her seat.

It was my turn.

I walked to the lectern. It felt like I was walking underwater. People clapped and it sounded like the waves crashing at the beach. I grabbed my opening remarks from my pocket and laid them on the lectern. I looked at Bec and Joe in the front row. Bec was holding a sign that said, "Vote for David Mortimore Baxter!" Joe gave me a thumbs-up.

Harry was next to Joe. He was busy making his seat's arms go up and down. Surprisingly, Zoe was there too. She sat next to Bec, looking bored.

I remembered my lesson with Zoe and grabbed the lectern with both hands.

I'd picked out something to look at the back of the hall. It was the large school flag. I talked to the flag, but **gradually I looked into the crowd**. I picked one person and talked straight to them. I pointed **my finger**. I **shook** my fist. **I was on a roll**.

When I was finished, I was pretty happy with myself.

Ms. Stacey stepped up to the lectern and threw some questions at us. I let Rose answer **first**. I was too busy figuring out which card answered Ms. Stacey's question. My answer cards **dropped onto the stage**, but Ms. Stacey didn't seem to notice. She was asking the audience for questions.

Rose's **GG's** were scattered through the audience. At least three of them got a question to Rose before Joe asked me anything.

"David, will you be banning **Smashing Smorgan pencil cases** if you become class president?" he asked.

I stood up.

"I most certainly will not," I said, thumping my clenched fist into the palm of my other hand.

Ms. Stacey pointed at Jake Davern, but Mrs. Thornton started talking before Jake could open his mouth. "I have a question for David. David, do you believe that women . . . girls . . . should have an equal right to become class president?" she asked firmly.

I looked down at Joe. He **shrugged** his shoulders. I looked at Bec and suddenly had an answer.

"I believe, Mrs. Thornton, that class president should be the best person for the job, boy or girl."

"I have a question for David," came a voice from the back of the hall.

It was Kaya, Rose's campaign manager. "David, is it true that you wear your sister's clothes?" she asked loudly.

CHAPTER 11

STIRRING THINGS UP

The hall fell **silent**. I stood up with a smile on my face. This was definitely something I had planned for.

"I only wear **one** of her dresses," I said firmly. "Some people think it looks better on me than her. Next question?"

The hall ERUPTED into **laughter**. It seemed like everyone had decided my answer was a joke. Rose scowled at me.

Ms. Stacey ended question time. Rose got up for a few last words. She seemed a little mad, like things hadn't worked out the way she planned.

"If you vote for David Baxter tomorrow, you will be voting for confusion," she said firmly. Gran **booed** loudly. "A class president needs to be **fair**. To be **bold** yet **calm**. To be strong and able to make the right decisions. A class president needs to understand how to organize a class party. How to choose the right activity and the right food and drink."

She pointed to me, like I was on **trial for murder.**

"David Baxter is NOT the person for the job. The only person who can fulfill the job stands before you now. Vote for Rose Thornton!" she said loudly.

Rose's GG's clapped, yelled, and cheered like they were at a rock concert. Other people clapped politely. A few booed again. Rose returned to her seat.

I grabbed my debate speech notes from the floor. I went to the lectern and waited for the noise to calm down. I looked at the things that Joe had written. **Leadership. Helping. Concern.** I grabbed the lectern with both hands and cleared my throat. I looked down at my notes again.

"If you vote for me tomorrow," I began. I tried looking at just one person in the crowd. That person just happened to be **Luke Firth** with his shiny class president badge. He nodded and smiled at me.

"If, if you," I stuttered. Rose laughed. All I could think of was that last thing Luke had said to me. Why did I want to be class president? The fact was, I didn't want to be.

"If you vote for me tomorrow," I continued, "you'll be voting for the **wrong person**."

A GASP ran through the crowd. People began talking. I held up my hands and the hall fell silent.

"These are the things I think a good class president should be," I said. Then I read out the speech that Joe had written.

". . . honesty," I finished. "If this is what you are looking for in a class president, then the person you should be voting for is LUKE FIRTH!"

People began talking loudly.

"Quiet, please," said Ms. Stacey.

I could see Mr. Woods making his way to the stage. I didn't have long before he'd take over the microphone.

"**Luke Firth** is our class president now," I babbled. "He has been class president all year and he's really good at it. Everybody likes him. He was going away and now he's not, and I think that he should still be class president because he's the best person for the job."

"If we have to have an election tomorrow," I added, "I'm asking you to vote for **Luke Firth**. Because I don't want the job."

This time the crowd went **wild**. Everybody looked at Luke Firth. People were yelling. Ms. Stacey was standing on the side of the stage. Her arms were crossed and she had this strange look on her face, like she was happy or something. Rose Thornton stood up. I was glad there were a lot of people around. She looked like she could STRANGLE me with her bare hands.

* * *

Mr. Woods had made it to the stage. He was talking quickly to Ms. Stacey, who was nodding her head.

I looked down at the front row. Joe and Bec both looked stunned. Zoe was smiling and clapping (I was shocked). Harry was holding his nose with one hand and giving me the **thumbs-down** with the other. Gran was standing, pounding her stick on the floor.

Mom was making her way over to Mrs. Thornton, who seemed to be CRYING.

Mr. Woods finally took the microphone.

"You certainly **know how to stir things up,**" he muttered to me.

CHAPTER 12

AND THE WINNER IS . . .

Mr. Woods was pretty good at calming everyone down. He explained about the change in Luke's plans. "I have talked with Ms. Stacey, and we've decided who the class president will be," he said.

A BUZZ ran through the room. Mrs. Thornton had stopped sobbing. For the first time I noticed Victor Sneddon. He looked like a sad puppy, all droopy and dull. I realized that he had just lost his chance at getting a date with Zoe. I figured I'd better stay out of his way for the rest of my life.

Mr. Woods waited for quiet, then continued.

"The class president for Ms. Stacey's grade for the rest of the year . . ."

A loud HICCUP came from the audience. I think it was Mrs. Thornton.

". . . is Luke Firth . . ."

There were SCREAMS from the crowd. Some happy, some not.

". . . and Rose Thornton."

What?

The crowd went crazy. Joe and Bec **hadn't moved** since I'd **announced** I wasn't running for class president.

I looked over at Rose. She looked CONFUSED. Mr. Woods asked Luke Firth to come to the stage. Luke and Rose walked to the lectern.

Rose **pushed Luke out of the way.** "Thank you very much," she gushed. "I can't believe it." It was like she'd won an **Academy Award** or something.

Luke moved forward, but Rose PUSHED him away. "I just need to thank a few people," she continued. "I'd like to thank Kaya, my campaign manager." She clapped and people followed her lead.

"I'd like to thank my poster people, my speech writers." There was some more clapping.

"**My heart goes out** to David Mortimore Baxter for losing," she said seriously. Then she turned to me and clapped again.

LOSING? I'd just given the class president position to Rose on a plate.

"And a big thank you to Luke for sharing this position with me."

That time there was real applause.

"Finally . . ."

I yawned.

"I'd like to thank all those people who believed in me. You know who you are," she said, pointing to the audience.

I followed her finger and saw Mrs. Thornton sobbing again.

Mr. Woods finally got Rose away from the microphone. "And now a few words from our co-class president winner, Luke Firth," he said.

Luke stood up to the microphone. He pulled it down so he could reach it.

"Thank you," he said.

The crowd went WILD. I slipped away through the side curtain.

I walked to the nurse's office. Mrs. Schtick, our school nurse, was **grumbling** as usual. She was busy trying to count all the things that were in her medicine cabinet.

"You don't need a bandage, do you?" she asked, shaking her fluffy hair at me. "I just counted those."

"No, Mrs. Schtick," I said. "I think I just need to lie down."

"I just made that bed," she said **grumpily**.

I promised not to mess it up.

I lay down and thought about the good things and the bad things about not being class president. It was getting confusing. I grabbed a piece of paper from Mrs. Schtick's desk and a pencil from the shelf and wrote it out.

Good Things

I won't have to stand up and make speeches.

Luke Firth gets to keep his class president badge

I won't have to stay in during lunchtime and do class president stuff.

I won't have to set a good example.

I won't have to keep any of my promises.

Joe might stop being so serious.

Bad Things

Rose Thornton will have to stand up and make speeches.

I won't get a shiny badge to wear.

Rose might ban Smashing Smorgan pencil cases.

Rose Thornton will get me in trouble with Ms. Stacey when I don't set a good example.

Some people might be mad at me because I don't have to keep any of my promises.

I might spend a lot of time on the hot seat because I'm late for school.

Ms. Stacey finally FOUND me.

"There are a whole lot of people that want to see you," she said with a **smile**.

I bet there are, I thought.

I SHOVED the list in my pocket.

"Okay," I said.

CHAPTER 13

A SURPRISE

It turned out that Ms. Stacey's surprise had been a PARTY after the debate. There was **a lot of food**, mostly donated by Mrs. Thornton. There was fruit punch and a **large cake with the words Congratulations David Mortimore Baxter** on it. How embarrassing.

"I made it," said Gran. "It took me a whole day, so you'd better have some."

"I'm sorry about not being class president, Gran," I said.

"**Nonsense**," said Gran. Then she bashed her way to the drink table.

I found Bec and Joe. Joe was stuffing as many marshmallows into his mouth as he could. It seemed like my campaign manager had left, leaving my crazy friend behind.

"Sixteen," counted Bec. "Seventeen."

"**Hi**," I said. "**Do you forgive me?**"

"Hey, sure," said Bec.

"But all that **work you did**," I said.

Bec shrugged. "I like doing that stuff. And I'll get graded for it anyway."

Joe was moving his mouth but I couldn't understand a word he said.

"I'll get him some PUNCH," said Bec.

The punch didn't work. There was **no room** in Joe's **mouth** for anything else. Joe finally went outside and cleared his mouth. When he came back, I didn't ask where it all went.

"**Hey**," he said.

"Hey, yourself."

We stood there looking around.

"I just want to say," I began.

"David, I," said Joe at the same time.

"You first," I said.

"David, I think I might have been a little out of control," said Joe.

"All those PROMISES we made? All those things we said about Rose?" Joe said.

"I know," I said.

"I knew you didn't want to be class president," said Joe. "But I pushed you."

"Next time I'll tell you to back off," I said.

"It's just that I really enjoyed being a campaign manager. People looked up to me. I had . . ."

"Power?" I asked.

"A briefcase," said Joe.

Rose SLITHERED up, looking a little distracted. "Hello," she said. She was dragging Luke behind her.

Joe nudged me. Maybe he thought I should apologize to Rose?

"I just wanted to say that things are really going to change around here. I'm keeping my eye on all three of you," she began.

"Which eye?" asked Joe.

"And you WON'T be getting away," said Rose.

"You'd really need **three eyes**," said Joe. "That would make it easier."

"—with anything," finished Rose.

I changed my mind about making an **apology**.

Rose walked off and left Luke, who looked confused.

"She can't ban Smashing Smorgan pencil cases, can she?" I asked.

"I'll TRY to keep her in line," said Luke. "And, **David, thanks**."

"Sure," I said.

Rose came back and dragged Luke away. "I can't get my SURPRISE finale to work," she complained.

"Poor Luke," said Bec.

Then Mom and Gran and Zoe and Harry walked over. They all were talking at once. I think they thought I'd done the right thing. Except Harry, of course. Then Mom pulled Harry and me aside.

"What's been going on with the chores at home?" she demanded. "I noticed that Harry seemed to be doing your chores, David. Then today I got a call from Mr. McCafferty. He got home this afternoon to find his prize roses WILTING."

"Harry!" I whispered.

"What?" he said. "There weren't **any roses** on your chores list."

He was right.

"David, you promised that you'd water Mr. McCafferty's garden. The **poor man** is beside himself," said Mom.

"I made a deal with Harry," I explained. "He was going to do all my chores."

"It was your PROMISE," said Mom. "It was up to **you** to keep it."

Jake Davern swung by and SMACKED me on the shoulder. Joe followed closely behind.

"I tried to explain, David," said Joe.

"So when do we get to **sponsor a monkey**?" Jake asked.

"We don't," I said. "That was only if I won the election."

"But that's not fair," said Jake.

"Look, that wasn't even a core promise," explained Joe. "It probably wouldn't have happened anyway."

I was trying to get Joe to stop talking. I didn't think Mom would understand about the election promises.

"Well, I'm sick of doing **David's chores**," Harry piped in. "I think he should do mine."

Then there was a large bang.

"It worked!" yelled Rose.

A whole cloud of balloons floated down from the ceiling. The balloons had Rose's face printed on them. I picked one up. She looked better with a green face.

"You and I need to have a **serious** talk, David Baxter" said Mom.

Jake stuck a balloon under the back of his sweater and was pretending to be a camel. Bec and Joe were bouncing balloons onto each other's heads. I found Luke in the crowd. He was picking up balloons, trying to make everything clean.

I loved not being class president.

"Yes, Mom," I said.

"And that's not a threat," she said, as a balloon drifted onto her head. "**That's a promise!**"

About the Author

When Karen Tayleur was growing up, her father told her many stories about his own childhood. These stories continued to grow. She says, "I always enjoyed the retelling, and wanted to create a character who had the same abilities with 'bending the truth.'" And David Mortimore Baxter was born! Karen lives in Australia with her husband, two children, two cats, and one dog.

About the Illustrator

Brann Garvey grew up in the great state of Iowa, where he studied art and visual communications. He graduated from the Minneapolis College of Art & Design with a degree in illustration. Brann is usually found with one or more of the following: a pencil in his hand, a comic book, a remote for watching DVDs, or his pet kitty, Iggy. When the weather is nice, Brann likes to play disc golf, and he proudly points out that Iowa is one of the world's centers for the sport. Iggy does not play.

Glossary

banning (BAN-ing)—forbidding

campaign (kam-PAYN)—an organized way of getting something done, such as an election

campaign manager (kam-PAYN MAN-uh-jur)—someone who is in charge of a campaign

candidate (KAN-duh-date)—someone who is running in an election

debate (di-BATE)—a discussion

democracy (di-MOK-ruh-see)—a form of government in which people vote

elect (i-LEKT)—to choose by voting

nominate (NOM-uh-nate)—to choose a candidate for election

opponent (uh-POH-nent)—someone who is against you in a contest (or election)

politician (pol-uh-TISH-uhn)—someone who has a position in the government

publicity (pu-BLISS-uh-tee)—information given out to get people's attention

victory (VIK-tuh-ree)—the winning of a contest or election

Discussion Questions

1. Do you feel that the process of nominating and electing a class president in this book was fair? Explain your answer. How does this process compare to the process of choosing leaders in your class or school?

2. How does Ms. Stacey feel about David Baxter's nomination? Give proof of this from the book.

3. Is a promise a promise? Discuss what Joe says to David about keeping promises on pages 17 and 18. Should you make promises to win an election? Should you keep those promises? Explain your thinking.

4. What ended up being fair in this book? What was unfair? Explain your answers.

Writing Prompts

1. How well do you know your classmates? Make
   a list of their names and what they are interested in.

2. Finish this sentence with your own thoughts and
   explanation: "A class president needs to
   be . . ."

3. David thinks about the good things and the bad
   things involved in being a class president and makes
   a list. Write your own list of what you think would
   be good and bad about being a class president.

4. Imagine that you've been nominated for class
   president. Write a speech describing how you would
   run your class, what promises you would make, etc.

STAYING OUT OF TROUBLE WITH DAVID MORTIMORE BAXTER

Manners!

DAVID MORTIMORE BAXTER
by KAREN TAYLEUR

STONE ARCH *Realistic Fiction*

SURVIVE AND SUCCEED WITH DAVID MORTIMORE BAXTER

DAVID MORTIMORE BAXTER
Excuses!
by KAREN TAYLEUR

STONE ARCH *Realistic Fiction*

DAVID MORTIMORE BAXTER COMES CLE

DAVID MORTIMORE BAXTER
The Truth!
by KAREN TAYLEUR

STONE ARCH *Realistic Fiction*

David Mortimore Baxter

David is a great kid, but he has one big problem—he can't
stop talking. These wildly humorous stories, told by David himself,
will show readers just how much trouble a boy and his mouth can
get into, whether he's making promises to become class president
or bragging that he's best friends with the world's most famous
wrestler. David is amiable, engaging, cool, and smart enough to
realize that growing up is the biggest adventure of all.

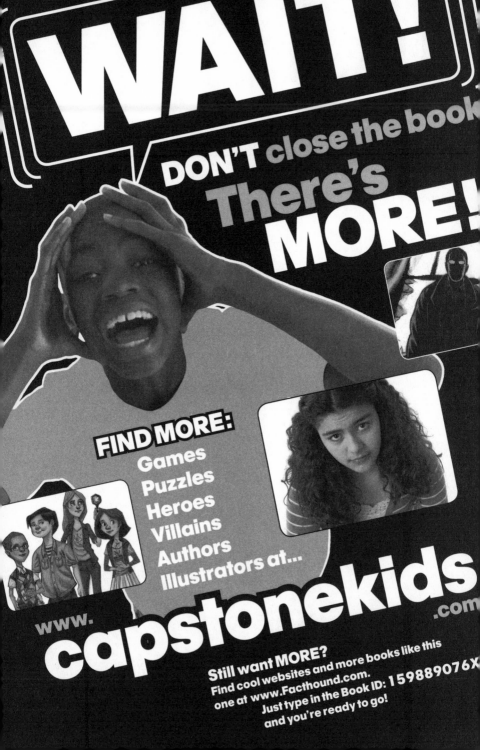